FIRST STEPS IN THE NCHANTED FOREST OF STITCHES

Peruchita lived with her family in a little house by the river, deep in the enchanted Forest of Stitches. Every morning she said good bye to her mother and walked to school along the path under the trees. As she went along she would look up at the branches to where the monkeys swung and the birds sang, and then to the river where the fish and the dolphins swam. And in her mind's eye she played a little game …

Words and Instructions
by
John & Bella Lane

Illustrated
by
Adebanji Alade

1

Peruchita
liked to imagine that the
flowers and the fruits and the big
leaves of the bananas and all the
creepers, and the distant clouds up above
running across the sky in the breeze were all
tied together by beautiful stitches like a
patchwork quilt. And when she got home in the
evening, she would choose one of the stitches and
draw a picture of what she had seen. Then she
would take her needle and her threads and work the
stitches into a special birthday present that she was
making for her mother ...

Running Stitch

(Monday's Stitch!)

Running stitch is one of the first hand-sewing or embroidery stitches to learn. Since ancient times it has been used to sew, repair and decorate pieces of cloth using needle and thread.

Running stitch:

As you read this book, *Peruchita* would like to invite you to start your very own first embroidery sampler. To do this, please open your embroidery kit inside the last page of this book.

Your Embroidery Kit Contains

1x piece of Aida fabric
2x skeins of red embroidery threads
1x tapestry needle
1x A4 picture of finished sampler

Threading the needle

Peruchita always follows her mother's advice on how to cut the perfect length of thread for her needle. Using her ruler she cuts 30cm long from the red skein of cotton thread.

Threading the needle:

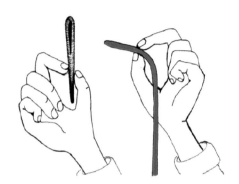

Then she threads the cotton through the eye of the needle (without licking the end of the thread!). She makes a fine knot at the end of her thread and she is ready to begin.

Tips to consider

Before any embroidery starts *Peruchita* washes her little hands and fingers with soap and clean water! As well, she reads very carefully the instructions given in this book and if she needs some extra help she always asks her mother for advice. On her sampler she starts her running stitch at the top of the fabric. See picture of the finished sampler.

Stitch Plan

As illustrated on the opposite page *Peruchita* remembers how the clouds had looked early that morning as they ran across the sky. In the same way she starts to stitch her running stitch from left to right, making a block of neat running stitches:

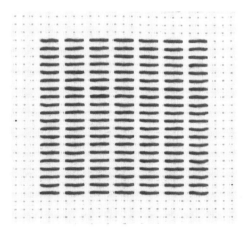

Peruchita is very pleased with her embroidery and now she is planning to make a secret present for her mother when the sampler is completed. What about you…?

Early next day Peruchita set o
for school once again. What a windy da
she thought to herself, that means rain is comin
All the leaves on the trees were busy whispering secre
to each other, and when she looked towards the river she sa
that little waves were dancing on the water. And as she watche
a fisherman passed in his canoe and an idea came to her for a ne
stitch to try that evening when she got hom

Back Stitch

(Tuesday's Stitch!)

Back stitch is one of the oldest and most useful stitches in the world. It is used not only by embroiderers but also by tailors, seamstresses, leather workers and in other crafts.

Traditional back stitch:

As well this stitch is extremely versatile. It can be worked in different ways, such as delicate straight lines, in varying sizes or even in circles. This stitch can be worked from left to right or right to left.

Tip

Peruchita remembers her mother's advice to wash her hands. This way her embroidery will keep clean and pristine.

Stitch Plan

In her sampler *Peruchita* works back stitch in a pyramid form, as it reminds her of the dancing waves on the water she saw that morning, as illustrated on the opposite page.

In five steps *Peruchita* works her back stitch from left to right.

Peruchita's 1st step:

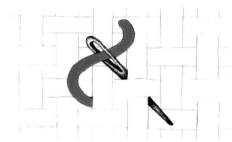

2nd step:

3rd step:

4th step:

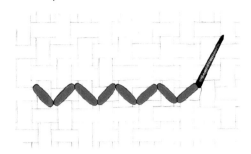

5th step:

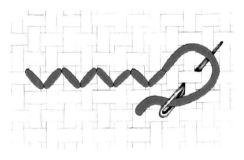

Bravo! Well done *Peruchita* !

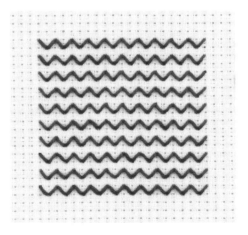

Her second block of stitches is ready...

Another day for school, another walk through the forest for Peruchita. And on that particular morning it was the beautiful parrots sitting in a row on a branch high up above her head that caught Peruchita's eye. She stopped to watch them on their perch, and as they chattered away and laughed at her, a thought came into Peruchita's head …

Cross Stitch

(Wednesday's Stitch!)

Cross stitch is a very popular decorative stitch, used in different ways all over the world.

Cross stitch is done by counting the threads on the fabric, the same as you are using for your embroidery.

Stitch Plan

And once more, as for the previous stitches, *Peruchita* looks at the back cover of this book to position her new cross stitch block in the right place on her sampler.

Following three simple steps, *Peruchita* works her cross stitch from right to left

1st step of cross stitch:

2nd step:

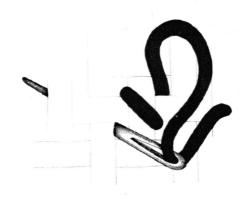

3rd step:

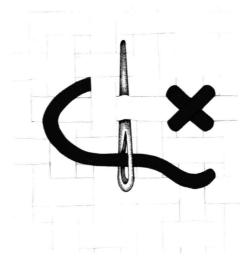

Line of cross stitch:

Nearly there…and now below the block of cross stitches is completed!!!

Peruchita is ready for bed!

'Take care dear,' said Peruchita's mother when she set out for school the next day, 'I think the rain is coming very soon.' And sure enough, Peruchita was hardly halfway to school when big black clouds appeared over the tree tops and it poured and poured. All the flowers and all the plants were so happy to have a drink. But Peruchita was not so pleased and quickly she took shelter under a big clump of banana trees. And as she watched the rain falling in straight lines running down the glistening leaves, she knew straightaway what stitch she would do when she got home that evening.

8

Boro Stitch

(Thursday's Stitch!)

Boro stitch is a free-hand stitch which has been used for generations on patches to mend old garments in Japan. Today these repaired garments are appreciated as unique art pieces for their age and simplicity, and 'story telling' about their owners.

Stitch diagram:

Tips

The stitches are free-hand, with long and short stitches.

Be creative with your stitches but be artistic, as the end result of this work needs to look like drops of rain in the forest.

Stitch plan

Peruchita starts her work from the top to the bottom, just like the rain-drops on the leaves.

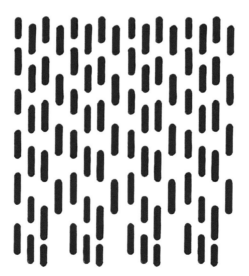

Wow! *Peruchita* is very pleased with her boro stitch:

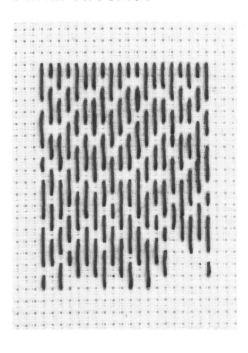

It does indeed look just like the rain!

The last day of the week for
school, and as Peruchita hurried
along the path under the trees she
thought about her mother's birthday,
which was on Saturday, the very next
day. Peruchita needed just one more
stitch to finish the pattern on her
needlework sampler, and she wondered
and wondered what it could be. Just then a
family of alligators passed by, and the Daddy
alligator smiled at her so sweetly and waved his
scaly tail to say Hi! And immediately Peruchita
knew the very stitch that she would work that
night when she got home.